KINDERGATORS

Hands Off, Harry!

. . . .

ROSEMARY WELLS

KATHERINE TEGEN BOOKS
An Imprint of HarperCollins Publishers

"Guess what happened at school today!"

"Tell us, Lola. . . ."

Harry ran all the way down the hall and into school backward!

He even said "Good morning" backward!

He knocked Babette, Tina, and Benjamin out of Friendly Circle and onto the floor!

Harry laughed, but no one else did.

Miss Harmony said it was not a friendly thing to do to Friendly Circle. She gave Harry a time-out in the Thinking Chair.

"Harry, you need to think about respecting other people's personal space," said Miss Harmony.

But Harry did not do too much thinking.

Babette told Miss Harmony, "Harry is disrespecting the Thinking Chair!" Miss Harmony redirected Babette to the bead corner.

You would think the Thinking Chair would make Harry think
about what he did wrong, but no!

At make-a-snowflake time he
sneaked out of his chair.

Then he poked Miracle in the ribs.

Her glue spilled onto her shoes
and ruined her snowflake.
Miracle melted down.

"It was an accident!" said Harry.
Everyone knew that wasn't the truth.
Harry got another time-out.

Miss Harmony rang her "listen up" bell.

"What do we use our hands for?" she asked.

"Shake a hand!" said Nigel.

"Hold a hand!" answered Babette.

"Lend a hand!" shouted Miguel.

Shake a hand

Hold a hand

Lend a hand

Do you think Harry thought about shaking, holding, or lending a hand?

ABCDEFGHIJKLMNO

No way!

While Miss Harmony was not looking, Harry scooted over to Benjamin's busy station. Harry put both hands on Benjamin's shoulders and shouted, "Surprise!"

Benjamin's poster paint spilled all over his new shirt and pants.

Miss Harmony had to wash Benjamin's clothes.

Then she got out Benjamin's cubby outfit.

Benjamin's cubby outfit didn't fit anymore.

I bet you'd think Miss Harmony got mad.
But no!
She rang her "listen up" bell and called for Friendly Circle.
Everyone got a turn to speak.
"We don't like to be pushed!" said Tina.

"Or poked!" said Babette.

"Hands off, Harry!" said Raúl.

"My favorite shirt is ruined forever!" said Benjamin.

"That snowflake was a present for my mama," said Miracle, "and now my shoes are stuck to my socks and my socks are stuck to my feet!"

"What should you say to your classmates, Harry?" asked Miss Harmony.

"Sor-reee!" said Harry.

"He doesn't mean it!" said Babette. "He's not using an *I'm sorry* voice."

"Harry," said Miss Harmony, "when you use your *I'm angry* voice to say 'I'm sorry,' no one believes you!"

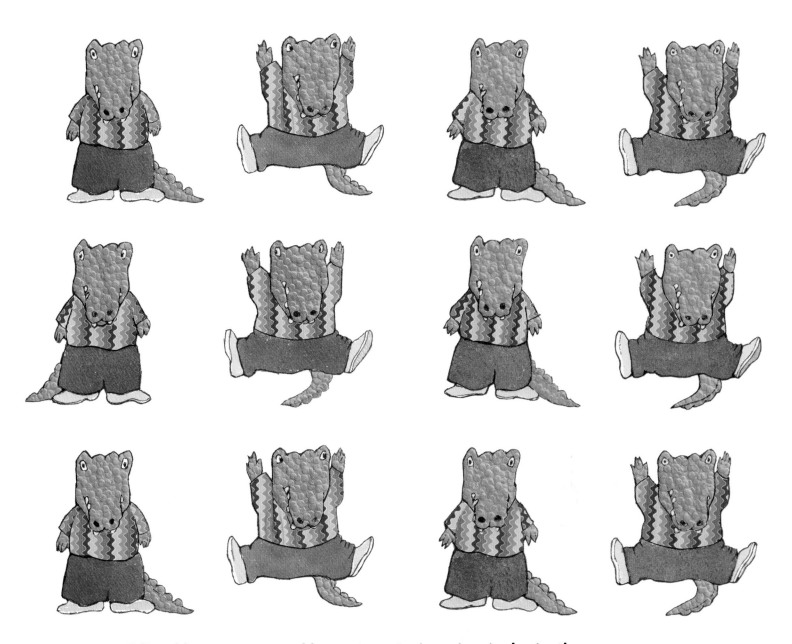

Miss Harmony gave Harry twenty jumping jacks in the corner.

"You have ants in your pants, Harry!" said Babette.

Miss Harmony redirected Babette to the dress-up corner.

But the ants stayed right in Harry's pants.

During yoga, Harry tackled Nigel.

Nigel's glasses snapped in two.

Friendly Circle was called into emergency session.

"Harry, you've invaded my personal space!" said Nigel.

Friendly Circle voted that Harry needed to learn where his space ended and where everybody else's began.

Just then, Babette had a brilliant idea!
She ran to the gymnasium.

Babette came back with the bumper tube from the
bouncing set. It was the perfect way for Harry to learn
about personal space because he couldn't reach anybody!

At snack time, Harry couldn't grab anyone's apple juice.

He couldn't join hands at sing-a-long.

Harry had *a lot* of time to think about personal space.

But guess what? At presentation time, Harry asked Miss Harmony to let him do his show-and-tell.

"What is your show-and-tell presentation, Harry?" asked Miss Harmony.

"I want to show everybody that my space ends here," said Harry. "I want to tell everyone I'm sorry."

Harry used his real *I'm sorry* voice.
"I think he means it!" said Miracle.

"Who's going to be playground monitor
today?" asked Miss Harmony.
"Please, me?" Harry asked Miss Harmony.
Everybody said, "No way! Not Harry!"

But Miss Harmony said, "Let's give Harry a chance."

And you know what?

Harry didn't touch anyone until Jazzmin fell off the walkathon bars.

Jazzmin howled and yowled so loud, you could hear her all the way downtown and all the way uptown.

But Harry was a good playground monitor.

He got out the first-aid kit. He cleaned Jazzmin's knees with a Steriwipe and put on two purple glitter Band-Aids. He even gave her a tissue to wipe her tears.

"Harry, you used your hands to help, not hurt!" Miss Harmony said. "I'm proud of you!"

Everyone got an oatmeal-raisin cookie. And guess what happened *then*?

Just before see-you-later-alligator time, Miss Harmony gave Harry the good-behavior gold star.

"And that's what happened
at school today!"

Creating Classroom Harmony

In my seventeen years as an educator in New York—at Public School 103 and currently as a first grade teacher at Little Red School House & Elisabeth Irwin High School—I am reminded each day of the importance of showing our students how to successfully engage in real-life problems. With guidance, children can and will work together to master their own behaviors, acquire gentle language, and respect personal space. (I happen to know Miss Harmony very well.)

When we teach children to care about one another and their classroom community, they will learn a habit of meaningful conversation and interaction. This book is designed to show how to help children become the kind of people we want them to be—thoughtful citizens of our increasingly complex world.

Here are some ideas about how to open a meaningful conversation about personal space:

- Before beginning, *talk about* the title and front cover. Invite readers to predict what they think the story will be about.

- While reading, ask readers to *stop* and *think* about why Harry could not keep his hands to himself. Ask them, "Do you know someone who is like Harry?" Listen as readers share about how parts of the story are similar to their lives or experiences and how other parts are different.

- *Discuss* the characters. Ask young readers, "How can you tell that Harry felt sorry about what he had done?" Encourage children to talk about things that surprised them in the story, or new things they learned.

- *Encourage* children to problem solve. Ask them, "How can we respect personal space? How will we know if we are taking care of one another's personal space?"

- *Create* opportunities for children to think about personal space. Ask them, "Why it is important to use your hands to help and not to hurt?"

—Gina Goldmann, classroom teacher

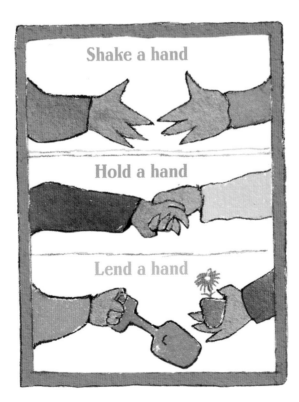

Thank you,
Johanna Hurley!

Thanks to Windham Fabrics, Maywood Studio Fabrics, RJR Fabrics, Moda Fabrics, Darlene Zimmerman, Judy Rothermel, Kaye England, and Barbara Brackman.

Katherine Tegen Books is an imprint of HarperCollins Publishers.

Library of Congress Cataloging-in-Publication Data: Wells, Rosemary. Hands off, Harry! / written and illustrated by Rosemary Wells.—1st ed.   p.   cm.—(Kindergators)
Summary: Harry has trouble keeping his hands off his classmates until Babette thinks of the perfect piece of gym equipment to teach him about personal space.
ISBN 978-0-06-192112-4 (trade bdg.) — ISBN 978-0-06-192113-1 (lib. bdg.)
[1. Alligators—Fiction.   2. Behavior—Fiction.   3. Interpersonal relations—Fiction.   4. Kindergarten—Fiction.   5. Schools—Fiction.]   I. Title.
PZ7.W46843Han 2011   [E]—dc22   2010016046   CIP   AC

Typography by Rachel Zegar   19 20   SCP   10 9 8 7 6 5 ❖ First Edition

Benjamin Miracle Nigel Babette Tina Lola